the CRitteR club

:0: Amy Meets Her Stepsister :0:

WITHDRAWN

by Callie Barkley 💙 illustrated by Marsha Riti

LITTLE SIMON

New York London Toronto Sydney New Delhi

LITTLE SIMON

An imprint of Simon & Schuster Children's Publishing Division 1230 Avenue of the Americas, New York, New York 10020 Copyright © 2013 by Simon & Schuster, Inc. All rights reserved, including the right of reproduction in whole or in part in any form. LITTLE SIMON is a registered trademark of Simon & Schuster, Inc., and associated colophon is a trademark of Simon & Schuster, Inc. For information about special discounts for bulk purchases, please contact Simon & Schuster Special Sales at 1-866-506-1949 or business@simonandschuster.com. The Simon & Schuster Speakers Bureau can bring authors to your live event. For more information or to book an event contact the Simon & Schuster Speakers Bureau at 1-866-248-3049 or visit our website at www.simonspeakers.com. Designed by Laura Roode

Manufactured in the United States of America 0719 MTN

20 19 18 17 16 15 14 13 12 11

Library of Congress Cataloging in Publication Data Barkley, Callie. Amy meets her stepsister / by Callie Barkley ; illustrated by Marsha Riti. —1st ed. p. cm. — (The critter club ; #5) Summary: Amy so looks forward to meeting her future stepsister, Chloe, that she is not prepared when Chloe first ignores her, then is downright mean. [1. Remarriage—Fiction. 2. Stepsisters—Fiction. 3. Clubs—Fiction. 4. Animal shelters—Fiction.] I. Riti, Marsha. II. Title. PZ7.B250585Anm 2013 [Fic]—dc23 2012042572

ISBN 978-1-4424-8215-9 (pbk)

ISBN 978-1-4424-8216-6 (hc)

ISBN 978-1-4424-8217-3 (eBook)

Table of Contents

Chapter 1

Big, Exciting News!

Amy Purvis's mom grabbed a pot-holder. She lifted the pot lid. Amy took a sniff.

"Mmmm," Amy said. "That smells *so* good!"

Inside the pot was a big batch of their famous chicken noodle soup. They had made it together. "The perfect dinner for a cool night,"

1

Amy's mom said with a smile.

Amy giggled. "Mom, this batch will last us all year!" It *was* a lot of soup for just the two of them.

Amy set the table. She put out two napkins and two soup spoons. Meanwhile, Amy's mom ladled soup into bowls.

Just as they sat down to eat, the phone rang.

"Start without me!" said Amy's mom, popping up to answer it.

Amy slurped up some broth and noodles. Right away, she felt warm all over.

"Oh, hi, Eliot!" she heard her mom say into the phone.

Amy's face lit up. Eliot was her father. He lived in Orange Blossom, a big town near Santa Vista. Even though her parents were divorced,

Amy got to see her dad a lot.

"Uh-huh," her mom was saying into the phone. "I bet she would love that!" She looked over at Amy and smiled. "Why don't you ask her?" Her mom held out the phone to Amy. "Your dad has a question for you," she said.

Amy jumped up and took the phone.

"Hi, Dad!" she said excitedly. "What's up?"

"Hey, kiddo," came her dad's voice through the phone. "How would you like to spend this weekend at my house?"

"Really?" said Amy. She loved her weekends with her dad. "But I thought that was *next* weekend."

"I know," her dad said. "But I've got some really big and exciting news to tell you."

News? "What is it?" Amy asked.

"You know what? I want to tell you in person," her dad said. "Oh! And Julia is going to come visit on Saturday too."

Julia was Amy's dad's girlfriend. He had met her about a year ago. Amy really liked Julia. She still kind of wished her mom and dad were married. But since *they* didn't want that, Amy was happy her dad had

met someone as nice as Julia.

"So I'll pick you up tomorrow. Okay?" her dad said.

"Okay! Bye!" said Amy, and she hung up the phone. She was so glad she wouldn't have to wait too long for the weekend. Tomorrow was Friday!

Then it hit her. *Friday.* It was sleepover night with her three best friends: Marion, Ellie, and Liz. They had one almost every week.

With a pang of disappointment, Amy flopped down into her

chair. "Oh, no. This means I can't go to the sleepover at Marion's."

Amy's mom patted her on the back. "You'll have fun with your dad, sweetie. And when we host

next week's sleepover, we can make it extra special."

Amy nodded. *And besides,* she thought, *we have lots of sleepovers. But how often does Dad have big, exciting news?*

Now she was really curious. What *was* the big news?

Chapter 2

A Lunchtime Mystery

Amy couldn't wait for school the next day. She wanted to tell her friends about her weekend with her dad—and the mystery news! Lunchtime was their first chance to talk.

"Maybe your dad is going to run for president!" Ellie said excitedly. Her brown eyes twinkled. "Or he is going to Hollywood to be in movies! Or he found out you're related to the Queen of England!"

Amy giggled. Ellie just loved the idea of being famous!

Marion slurped the last of her

HOLLYWOOD

chocolate milk. "Maybe he will take you on a shopping spree!" she suggested.

Then Liz spoke up. "Maybe your dad wants to write about The Critter Club in his newspaper!"

The Coastal County Courier

The Critter Club!

Hmmm . . . , thought Amy. That was a possibility. Amy's dad was the editor of a newspaper called *The Coastal County Courier*. He knew all about The Critter Club. It was the animal shelter that the girls ran in their friend Ms. Sullivan's barn.

"That could be it," said Amy. "My dad did say one time that it would make a good story—how the club got started."

And it actually *was* a good story. Before the four girls really knew Ms. Marge Sullivan, they had helped her find her missing

puppy, Rufus. Then Ms. Sullivan had a great idea. She decided Santa Vista needed an animal shelter to help lost and stray animals. Ms. Sullivan had an empty barn, and the girls had a love of animals, and that's how it all began!

The
Critter
Club

It helped that Amy's mom was a veterinarian. Dr. Purvis taught the girls how to take care of the different animals that had been at The Critter Club so far:

bunnies, kittens, dogs— even a turtle and a tarantula!

"Well, I am sorry I won't be around this weekend," Amy said. "I wanted to help out with the eggs."

They were incubating a dozen chicken eggs at The Critter Club.

A local farmer had dropped them off a week before. His family had to move. They had sold or given away most of their farm animals.

Then, before their move, their best hen had laid a clutch of eggs. But she didn't want to sit on them. Amy's mom said sometimes hens did that.

Luckily, the farmer knew about The Critter Club. He had brought the eggs and the incubator. The

girls were so excited to help them hatch. Then they would find the chicks new homes!

"Don't worry," said Liz. "We can handle the eggs. They're not due to hatch for another week."

"But we will miss you at the sleepover tonight!" Marion said. She put an arm around Amy's shoulders.

"Oooh! And call one of us when you get the good news!" Ellie begged. "I can't wait to hear it!"

Chapter 3

Dinner with Dad

The drive from Amy's house to her dad's only took about twenty minutes. But in that time, Amy had asked him the same question ten times.

"*Now* can you tell me the big, exciting news?" she asked again. They were pulling into his driveway.

Her dad shook his head for the

eleventh time. "Nope! You'll have to wait until dinner!" he said. "First let's get you settled in. Then we're going out."

We're going out to dinner? Amy thought. *This* is *a big deal.*

Amy walked into her dad's house, thinking once again how cool it was. The walls were painted bright colors. The furniture was simple and square. Her dad said the style was called "modern." His house

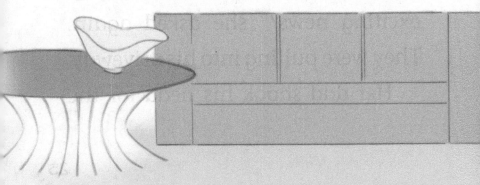

was so different from her mom's house, which was very cozy but not as colorful.

The art on her dad's walls was also really bright. *I've got to bring*

Liz here sometime, Amy thought. Liz was an amazing artist. *Maybe she can tell me what these are.*

Amy loved that she had her very own room at her dad's house. She plopped her heavy backpack down

on her bed. Then she unpacked. She had a huge pile of books. She had brought the newest Nancy Drew mystery, plus *The Wind in the Willows*, *Black Beauty*, and *The Wonderful Wizard of Oz*.

"Hungry?" her dad asked as he poked his head into Amy's room.

Amy nodded.

So off they went to dinner. It was a short walk to Amy's favorite

restaurant in Orange Blossom—
The Library. The walls were wall-
papered with old book pages. The
menu was Amy's favorite part.

The Library

Starter: The Secret Garden Salad

Appetizer: The Mad Hatter's
Tea Sandwiches

Entree: 20,000 Leagues Under
the Seafood Sampler

Amy and her dad ordered. When
the waiter had gone, her dad smiled
across the table.

"I have a pile of old newspapers we can cut up," he told her.

"Cool!" Amy exclaimed.

Amy and her dad loved creating poems together. They cut words out of newspapers or magazines. They moved them around until they had a poem they liked.

Then they glued the words to a piece of paper.

"And, hey! What's going on with The Critter Club?" her dad went on.

Amy told him all about the eggs that were going to hatch. But she really wanted to talk about some-thing else.

"Dad, wasn't there some big news?" Amy said. She looked at him and squinted. "It's dinnertime. Can you tell me *now*?"

Her dad smiled. "Okay, you're

right," he said. "Well, Julia is going to come over tomorrow."

"Right," said Amy. "You told me on the phone." She and her dad and Julia always had fun together.

"And Julia's going to bring some-one with her," her dad went on. "Do you remember that Julia has a daughter? Her name is Chloe."

Amy nodded. She remembered. Julia talked about Chloe a lot. Amy had never met her because Chloe was often away visiting her dad in Arizona. Amy felt the slightest flutter of butterflies in her stomach. Amy was shy about meeting new people. *But Julia is nice*, she thought. *I bet Chloe will be nice too.*

"She's eight years old, just like you are!" her dad continued.

"And . . . here's the really big news: the reason we'd love you and Chloe to finally meet is that Julia and I are engaged!"

Engaged? Amy's face flushed a little. "Like, getting married?" she asked.

Her dad nodded. "That's the idea," he said. "We haven't set a date yet. But we'd like to get married someday—maybe next year."

"Oh," was all Amy could think of to say. Her mind was racing. *If Dad and Julia get married, will Julia be my stepmom? And what about Chloe? Will she be my . . . stepsister?*

Now there were a million butterflies in Amy's stomach. They were fluttering around like crazy. She was really nervous about meeting Chloe.

What if we don't have anything in

common? Amy thought. *What if I don't like her? Or worse: what if she doesn't like me?*

Chapter 4

Chloe

The next morning, Amy woke up to the smell of pancakes. *Yum!* She got out of bed and put on her slippers. As she did, she remembered part of a dream she'd had. In it, she had been getting ready for a big fancy ball. Her dress was perfect. She was all set to leave. Then three mean stepsisters appeared and tore her beautiful dress to shreds.

Stepsisters, Amy thought. *I guess I really am nervous about meeting Chloe!*

Down in the kitchen, her dad was flipping pancakes. There was a place set at the table for Amy. Next to it was a stack of newspapers.

"Breakfast, coming right up!" her dad said. "Have a seat. I wrote you a poem."

Amy found the paper on the table, next to her fork.

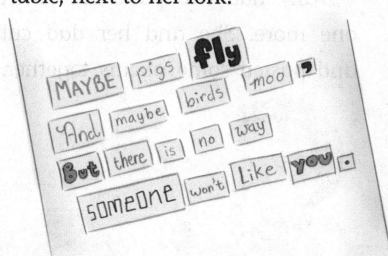

MAYBE pigs **fly**
birds moo,
And maybe
But there is no way
someone won't Like **you**.

Amy giggled. "Thanks, Dad," she said. It was like he could read her mind.

Her dad came over and gave her a kiss on the head. "Don't worry," he said. "You and Chloe will get along great."

Amy had two pancakes—then one more. She and her dad cut and pasted some poems together.

Then Amy went to her room to get dressed.

As she put on her shoes, she heard the doorbell. *Ding-dong!*

Amy took a deep breath. Then she walked toward the front hall.

Her dad was already at the door. At first, Amy could only see Julia on the front stoop. She looked the same as Amy remembered: shiny, straight black hair, sparkling brown eyes, and a big, friendly smile.

"Amy!" Julia said, spotting her. She breezed in and greeted Amy with a hug. "It's so good to see you. And I'm so happy for you to meet Chloe."

Julia stepped aside. Amy realized Chloe was standing right behind Julia. In fact, Chloe was holding on to the back of Julia's blue coat. Then, quickly, Chloe let go. She smiled at Amy.

Amy's first thought was: *She looks so much like her mom!* Chloe had the same shiny dark hair, but hers was in braids.

Her second thought was: *Ellie would love that outfit*. She had on a dark green dress and shiny black patent leather shoes. It reminded Amy of the pretty costumes Ellie liked to wear.

"Hi," said Chloe with a small wave.

"Nice to meet you," Amy said—and tried hard not to blush. It happened every time Amy felt shy or embarrassed. And at that moment, she was feeling both.

Chapter 5

A Messy Beginning

Julia held up a plastic container. "It's not too early for cookies, is it?" she asked, smiling. "I was hoping you girls could help me by decorating them."

Amy thought that sounded fun!

Amy's dad set the girls up at the kitchen table. Julia had made sugar cookies that were shaped like hearts

and stars. There were tubes of icing, sprinkles, and colored sugar. Julia put out a glass of water.

"For smoothing the icing," she explained.

Chloe sat down. Amy took the seat across from her.

"Julia and I are going to do some gardening out back," Amy's dad told the girls.

"Just give us a call if you need

us. Okay?" added Julia.

Chloe smiled at her mom. Amy nodded and took a cookie. Chloe did too.

Then, as their parents went out the back door, both girls reached for the tube of yellow icing.

"Oh!" said Amy. "It's okay. You take it. I'll use the blue."

Chloe didn't say anything. She just took the yellow. Then she scooted her chair a little farther from the table.

Why did she do that? Amy wondered. *Maybe she just needs more room to decorate. . . .*

She glanced over at Chloe. Chloe had her eyes locked on her cookie. For a few minutes, the kitchen was silent.

Is it possible? thought Amy. *Someone who's even shyer than I am?*

As shy as she was herself, Amy wanted to be a good hostess. "So, what school do you go to?" she asked Chloe.

At first, Chloe didn't answer. She was still staring at her cookie, squeezing out the yellow icing. But then she blurted out: "Orange Blossom School for Girls."

"Oh," said Amy. "I know where that is." She waited to see if Chloe had more to say.

She didn't.

So Amy said, "I go to Santa Vista Elementary."

Chloe didn't look up.

"My three best friends and I started an animal shelter," Amy went on. "It's called The Critter Club. We take care of strays and lost or hurt animals."

Chloe still didn't say anything.

"Do you like animals?" Amy tried.

For the first time since their parents had left, Chloe looked up. *"Ew,"* she said. Her face scrunched up, like she smelled something gross. "Animals are dirty and smelly. Why would you want to be around them so much?"

Amy felt her cheeks flush hot. She had no idea what to say to that.

Just then, Chloe reached for the pink icing. Her elbow knocked over the water glass. Water spilled onto the cookie plate, soaking the cookies.

Quickly Amy reached for a towel. "Oh, don't worry," Amy said. "It's not a big deal."

Then Amy's dad walked in the back door. "Forgot my gardening gloves," he said with a smile. "How's it going?"

Chloe jumped out of her seat. She pointed at Amy. "*She* did it!" Chloe shouted. "She knocked over the water! The cookies are ruined!"

Chapter 6

Fashion Disaster!

Julia and Chloe cleaned up the cookies while Amy helped her dad pull some weeds in the garden.

"Hey, is everything okay, kiddo?" Amy's dad asked her. "You're being awfully quiet."

Amy nodded. But everything *wasn't* okay. *Chloe really doesn't like me*, Amy thought. *Why else would she say I spilled the water?*

"Okay, change of plans!" Julia said, walking outside. Chloe was behind her. "Amy, Chloe and I were talking. How about we three girls go shopping?"

Amy looked at her dad. She gave him her

I-hate-to-shop face. He gave her his *Oh-come-on-it-might-be-fun* face.

"I'll meet you all at the park afterward," her dad said.

"There's a great new bookstore in town," Julia went on. "We could walk there."

"Yeah!" said Chloe. She was smiling. "That's right next to *my* favorite store. We could go to both!"

"Oh!" said Amy. Shopping for books? That *was* fun. *And it kind of seems like Chloe wants me to come.*

"Okay," Amy said. She smiled back at Chloe.

Maybe I was wrong. Maybe she doesn't hate me, after all.

They went to Chloe's favorite store first. It was a clothing store called Threads. As soon as they stepped inside, Chloe disappeared in the clothing racks. Julia waved to the lady at the register. They seemed to know each other. Julia went over to chat.

Amy was left alone. She felt like she was frozen in her spot. It was the

kind of store that made her feel . . . lost. Minutes crept by.

Then Chloe came rushing over. She already had an armload of clothes. "Amy! Come on! Let's try some things on," Chloe said.

"No, that's okay. You can go ahead—" Amy started to say.

But Chloe grabbed her hand. She

pulled Amy to the back of the store. "Look! These would look *so, so good* on you!" Chloe said.

She handed Amy some items on hangers. Then she shooed Amy into a dressing room. "I'll try some things on next door," said Chloe. "Meet out by the mirror in five!"

Before Amy knew it, the door was closed.

Amy sighed. She really didn't

like trying things on in stores! But Chloe was being so nice. How could she say no?

So Amy put on the clothing. She looked at herself in the mirror. *This can't be right,* she thought. *I've heard of mixing patterns like stripes and polka dots. But this is ridiculous. Isn't it?*

Amy thought about Liz. Her clothes were colorful and different—and she always got compliments on her outfits. So maybe Amy looked okay, after all.

Amy took a deep breath and opened the door. Chloe was standing by the mirror. She was wearing a daisy yellow party dress, purple ballet flats, and a sparkly headband. Her outfit was so pretty!

Amy walked over and stood next

to Chloe. They both looked in the mirror.

In a flash, Amy knew: her outfit was crazy with a capital C.

Then her eyes met Chloe's in the mirror. Amy could see it in Chloe's eyes. *She's trying not to laugh!*

Chloe had made her dress up like a fool.

"Oh, my," said a saleswoman, coming over to Amy. "Dear, *what* are you wearing?"

Amy ran back into the dressing room and closed the door.

Chapter 7

Amy to the Rescue

The trip to the bookstore wasn't much fun either.

At least *Julia* was being nice to Amy, as always. Julia showed Amy her favorite books from when she was a girl. Amy thought she'd like to read some of them.

Then Julia headed to the cookbook section. Chloe came over. "Hey,

Amy," she said. "Have you read these?" She held out a small pile of books. Amy reached out to take them.

Chloe let go before Amy had a grip. The books fell to the floor. *Thwump!* Other shoppers nearby turned to look. Amy's face flushed.

Was it just Amy's imagination, or had Chloe done that on purpose?

In the bookstore café, Julia got each girl a hot chocolate. While Julia paid, Amy headed to the counter. She reached for the cinnamon.

"Oh, I love cinnamon too!" said Chloe, appearing at Amy's side. She snatched up the cinnamon. "Here, let me!" She started sprinkling the cinnamon on Amy's hot chocolate.

"Thanks!" said Amy.

Chloe kept sprinkling.

"Okay!" Amy said. "That's great."

Chloe kept sprinkling.

"Chloe! That's enough!" Amy covered the top of her cup. Chloe finally stopped.

Amy sipped her hot chocolate. It was *way* too cinnamon-y.

Amy was glad when they met her dad in the park. He had brought a picnic for them.

"How was the shopping?" he asked Amy. They were tossing the Frisbee. Chloe and Julia were sitting together over on the picnic blanket.

Amy shrugged. "It—it was okay," she said glumly.

She had thought it would be such a fun weekend. But now she just missed Liz, Ellie, and Marion.

"Call us when you get the good news!" Ellie had said. Turned out it wasn't good news at all. Amy had a wicked stepsister!

Amy threw the Frisbee. The wind blew it a little off course. It glided toward the picnic blanket.

Out of nowhere, a dog came

running out of some bushes. It was chasing the Frisbee and barking like crazy.

Chloe saw the dog coming her way—and let out an ear-piercing scream! She jumped up and darted behind Julia.

Meanwhile, the Frisbee landed next to the blanket. The dog, a Dalmatian, ran right past it. Now the dog was more interested in Chloe! It ran up to her and barked.

Chloe screamed
again and ran behind
a tree.

The dog chased her, barking and
wagging its tail.

Chloe needed help. Amy ran
over. "Chloe," she said calmly. "It's

okay." Chloe looked terrified. "Trust me," Amy said. Then she turned to face the dog. The two girls stood side by side.

"Sit!" Amy said firmly.

The dog stopped barking and froze. Then it sat back on its hind legs.

"Stay!" Amy said.

The dog sat very still, watching Amy. It seemed to be waiting for another command.

Chloe turned to Amy. "Thank you!" she cried, and hugged her tight.

chapter 8

A New Friend?

"Nice going, kiddo," Amy's dad said, and patted her on the back.

Julia had an arm around Chloe, who still looked shaken up. "That was amazing," Julia said. "Thank you, Amy. Chloe is sometimes a little scared of animals."

Amy remembered what Chloe had said earlier about animals

being smelly and dirty. *Maybe she just didn't want to say she was afraid of them.*

"My mom has had Dalmatians at her vet clinic," Amy explained. "She told me that they have a lot of energy and are very playful. I think this dog just wanted to play with Chloe."

The dog—who was female—was still sitting quietly. She watched them talking.

"She doesn't have a collar or a tag," Amy noticed.

Amy's dad looked around. "I wonder if she got loose from her owner," he said.

Together, they walked around
the park. They didn't see anyone
who seemed to be looking for a dog.

Luckily, the Orange Blossom Animal Shelter was only two blocks away. They decided to take the dog over there. "We can see if anyone has reported her missing," Julia said.

They packed up their picnic basket. As they walked toward the shelter, the dog followed closely behind Amy. Chloe cautiously came up to walk by Amy's side.

"Thanks again, Amy," she said quietly. "You really helped me out."

"It was no problem," Amy said. "Really."

They walked along without talking for a minute. Then Chloe said, "I *was* listening before when you told me about The Critter Club. And that you started it with your three best friends. I have three best friends too. We have a jewelry-making club called the Sapphire Society."

"Cool!" said Amy. "That sounds fun!" She really meant it.

Chloe nodded. "And my mom says you like mysteries?"

Amy beamed. "I wouldn't go anywhere without a Nancy Drew," she told Chloe.

"Me too!" said Chloe.

Wow, thought Amy. *Maybe we do have* some *stuff in common.*

When they got to the Orange Blossom Animal Shelter, they led the dog inside. At the front desk, they met the owner, Mr. Beebe.

"Ah, yes," Mr. Beebe said. "The Dalmatian. I've been getting calls about you, young lady," he said to the dog.

The dog barked once, as if she understood. "I've heard she's been roaming around town for about a week now. We put up some flyers with her description. But we haven't

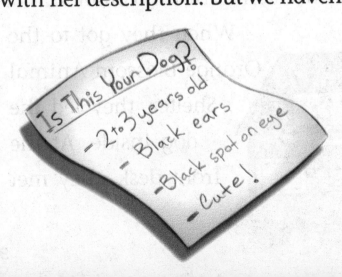

Is This Your Dog?
- 2 to 3 years old
- Black ears
- Black spot on eye
- Cute!

gotten a call from anyone looking for her," Mr. Beebe continued. "She must be a stray."

"Poor girl," said Julia, petting the dog's head. "She seems like she'd make a great pet for someone. What can we do to help her?"

Mr. Beebe sighed. "The problem is, we're pretty crowded right now," he said. "We have so many animals we need to find homes for. I don't suppose you folks know anyone who might be able to find her a good home?"

Amy smiled at her dad. Amy's dad smiled back.

"Mr. Beebe," said Amy, "I know just the place."

A look of understanding brightened Chloe's face. "The Critter Club!" she exclaimed.

Chapter 9

Heart-to-Heart

That evening back at the house, Amy, her dad, Chloe, and Julia were playing a board game.

"It was nice of Mr. Beebe to let Penny stay over tonight at the shelter," said Amy. Penny was the name they'd given the Dalmatian.

Amy's dad nodded. "And it was nice of your mom to agree to pick

Penny up tomorrow when she comes to get you," he said.

Dr. Purvis was even going to give the dog a checkup at her clinic. She wanted to make sure Penny was healthy before they took her to The Critter Club.

"How about some cookies for dessert?" Julia said.

"Yum!" cried Amy and Chloe together. They both laughed.

Amy's dad and Julia went to get the cookies. Chloe rolled the dice.

"You know what?" Chloe said. "I thought of one other thing we have in common."

"What?" said Amy.

"We're both only children," said Chloe. She moved her game piece. "I've always wanted a sister. But when my mom told me that she and your dad were going to get married . . . I don't know. I guess I started to worry about it. I was *super* nervous to meet you."

"Really?" said Amy. "To meet *me*?"

Chloe nodded. "I'm sorry for the way I acted," she said to Amy.

Amy smiled. "That's okay," she told Chloe. "I was really nervous

too. I was scared you wouldn't like me." Her cheeks flushed a little. "And then I was *sure* you didn't."

Chloe shook her head. "No, I just kept messing up! All day! I blamed you for spilling the water because, well, I didn't want your dad to be mad at me. I just really want him to like me. And at the clothing store, I was trying to be silly, not mean. But then I could tell you were upset and . . . I didn't know what to say."

Amy laughed.

Chloe also explained that she had tripped at the bookstore and accidentally dropped the books. And she hadn't been paying attention with the cinnamon. Chloe looked down. "I'm sorry I messed up your hot chocolate."

"It's really okay," Amy said. She felt so relieved. Her future stepsister wasn't mean, after all. "I guess we

act nervous in different ways. My face turns bright red. You do crazy stuff!"

Amy and Chloe giggled together. Then Amy had an idea.

"You have to come visit me in Santa Vista sometime!" she told Chloe. "I'll take you to The Critter

Club. We have some chicks that are going to hatch soon."

Chloe looked like she was thinking it over. "Chicks?" she said. "You mean like tiny, yellow, fluffy baby chickens?"

Amy nodded. "Yep. They don't bark at all!"

Chloe smiled. "That sounds great. You've got a deal."

chapter 10

More Big, Exciting News

On Sunday, Marion, Ellie, and Liz met Amy at The Critter Club. Amy and her mom had brought Penny over that morning. She seemed to be settling right in. She was already best friends with Rufus, Ms. Sullivan's dog. They ran and played together while Amy told her friends about the weekend. There

was so much to tell: about find-
ing Penny, about her dad getting
engaged, and all about Chloe!

"You guys will like her a lot,"
Amy said. "She likes pretty clothes
and jewelry—just like you, Marion."
Marion smiled. "She decorated her
cookies with lots of cool designs—
like you would, Liz."

"I like her already!" said Liz.

"And she really loves sparkles!" added Amy.

"Like me!" exclaimed Ellie. She twirled around in her sparkly dress. The girls giggled.

"Well, I'm excited to meet her," Marion said. "And I'm glad you're back, Amy."

"Yeah!" said Liz. "We missed you. *And* it's about to get pretty busy around here. Come see!"

She pulled Amy toward the egg incubator inside the barn. Amy gasped. There was a teeny, tiny beak poking out of a hole in one of the eggs.

"Surprise!" Ellie said.

"It started hatching yesterday," said Marion, "ahead of schedule."

"The others can't be far behind!" Liz added.

Amy clapped. "Amazing!" she exclaimed. She looked at the little chick peeking out at them. "You're the very first one! But your new brothers and sisters could hatch any minute now!"

Then Amy leaned in closer. She whispered something only the chick could hear: "Don't be nervous. I'm sure you guys will get along great."

Read on for a sneak peek at
the next Critter Club book:

#6

Ellie's Lovely Idea

Early on a Saturday morning, Ellie and her three best friends, Liz, Marion, and Amy, were making valentines in Amy's kitchen. The girls had slept over at Amy's house. They were still in their pajamas!

"Ten down, ten to go!" Ellie said, adding a valentine to her "done" pile. She smiled. Ellie loved seeing her name in sparkly red glitter!

Valentine's Day was coming up next Friday—less than a week away! There would be a party in their second-grade class. The girls were making valentines to give to their classmates.

"Valentine's Day is so much fun," said Liz as she finished up her second valentine. Liz was a true artist. She was taking lots of time on each card.

"February would be so boring without it," Marion agreed. She was using lots of ribbon. Each one of her cards looked like an award. Marion knew all about winning awards. She was really good at piano and ballet, and she was a great horseback rider.

"It *has* been a quiet month," said Amy. She was cutting and folding her cards into tiny books. "We haven't had any animals at The Critter Club for weeks!"

The Critter Club was the animal shelter that the four girls had started in their town of Santa Vista. Their friend Ms. Sullivan had come up with the idea after the girls had found her missing puppy. Ms. Sullivan had even let them take over her empty barn. Now it was The Critter Club! With the help of Amy's mom, a veterinarian, the girls cared for stray, lost, or hurt animals.

"That reminds me!" cried Amy. "We got a photo from the woman who adopted Penny." Penny was a stray Dalmatian that the girls had been taking care of—until a few weeks ago. Together they had found the perfect home for her.

Amy got the photo from the kitchen. She came back and showed the girls.

Ellie sighed. "I sure do miss having her around The Critter Club." Amy, Liz, and Marion all nodded.

Just then, Amy's mom, Dr. Purvis, came in from the living room. "I couldn't help overhearing you girls while I was opening the mail," she said. "You know, just because there are no animals at the club doesn't mean you can't help some other animals."

Dr. Purvis dropped an open envelope onto the table. Then she winked and walked away.

Ellie reached for the envelope.

She pulled out the paper inside. Amy, Liz, and Marion looked over her shoulder.

"Oh! Puppy Love!" said Amy. "This is an organization that my mom's friend Rebecca started. That's her." Amy pointed to the woman in the photo. "She gives money to families who need help paying for their new puppy's medical care—like all the shots that keep a puppy healthy."

"It looks like Puppy Love is trying to raise more money," Marion pointed out.

Ellie looked at the cute puppies in the photo and smiled. *How much money do I have at home in my piggy bank?* she wondered. *Twelve dollars?* She would gladly donate it all to Puppy Love if it would help those families—and puppies—who needed it.

I just wish it could be more, she thought. *Much, much more.*

If you like **the CRITTER club** you'll love **HE·D· HECKELBECK**